Little Louie

Kathryn Finney

Sky Pony Press
New York

To all the Little Louies who
need a happy home.

—K. F.

Copyright © 2014 by Kathryn Finney

All rights reserved. No part of this book may be reproduced in any manner without the express written consent of
the publisher, except in the case of brief excerpts in critical reviews or articles. All inquiries should be addressed to
Sky Pony Press, 307 West 36th Street, 11th Floor, New York, NY 10018.

Sky Pony Press books may be purchased in bulk at special discounts for sales promotion, corporate gifts, fund-
raising, or educational purposes. Special editions can also be created to specifications. For details, contact the
Special Sales Department, Sky Pony Press, 307 West 36th Street, 11th Floor, New York, NY 10018 or info@
skyhorsepublishing.com.

Sky Pony® is a registered trademark of Skyhorse Publishing, Inc.®, a Delaware corporation.

Visit our website at www.skyponypress.com.

10 9 8 7 6 5 4 3 2 1

Manufactured in China, April 2015
This product conforms to CPSIA 2008

Library of Congress Cataloging-in-Publication Data

Finney, Kathryn Kunz, 1960- author, illustrator.
  Little Louie / Kathryn Finney.
     pages cm
  Summary: Louie is a special dog, clumsy and funny-looking, but he dreams of being a champion like his brothers
until the day he slips on his ball into the center ring and discovers that he can be a different kind of star.
  ISBN 978-1-62914-615-7 (hardback)
  [1. Dogs--Fiction. 2. Individuality—Fiction. 3. Self-Confidence—Fiction. 4. Dog shows—Fiction.] I. Title.
  PZ7.F49823Lit 2014
  [E]--dc23
  2014015996

Print ISBN: 978-1-5107-0301-8
Ebook ISBN: 978-1-63220-214-7

Cover design by Kathryn Finney
Cover illustration credit Kathryn Finney

Louie was a little dog.

His tongue almost always hung out of his mouth, his legs were a bit too long, and one of his ears always pointed up.

Little Louie had three brothers, and he wanted to be a champion just like them.

Little Louie would try to walk like his brothers

"Heel!"

and fetch like his brothers.

"Fetch!"

Unlike his brothers, Little Louie had different commands from his owner.

"Stay!"

Although Little Louie was small, he had a big dream.

Little Louie wanted to be a star.

He dreamed about it

when he was taking walks in the bright, warm sunlight.

He dreamed about it while sleeping.

And he dreamed about it when he was playing with his

favorite thing: his ball.

Little Louie not only dreamed of being a star when he chased his ball.

He also dreamed when he bounced,

and ran on top of it.

tossed,

But there was one trick with the ball that Little Louie hadn't mastered.

Little Louie dreamed about balancing on top of that ball. He practiced this trick over and over. He hoped this would make him a star, and that would make Little Louie very happy!

Little Louie knew he needed to learn to heel, fetch, and jump to be a star. But he loved playing with his ball most of all.

Little Louie always joined
his brothers at their shows.
He was their number-one fan.

But one day, when the announcer said, "Next up, the Australian Shepherd," Little Louie leaned around the curtain, still dreaming about his trick on top of his ball, and tried to get a closer look at his brothers.

But his paws slipped!

Little Louie spun

and twirled

and flopped without ever slipping off his ball.

He rolled into the center ring, and then,

Little Louie balanced!

The crowd was silent. You could hear a dog biscuit drop a mile away. Then Little Louie heard a clap. And then he heard more clapping. And then there was a roar of applause! At that moment, Little Louie realized something. He didn't have to be like his brothers to be happy or to be a star.

He just had to be Little Louie.

So Little Louie got on top of his ball

. . . and spun and twirled and tossed and balanced.

That made Little Louie happier than he had ever dreamed.